Morning Sounds, Evening Sounds

by **Cecile Schoberle**

illustrated by **Harvey Stevenson**

SIMON & SCHUSTER BOOKS FOR YOUNG READERS
Published by Simon & Schuster
New York   London   Toronto   Sydney   Tokyo   Singapore

"Wake up, honey," Mom calls from the doorway of my bedroom.

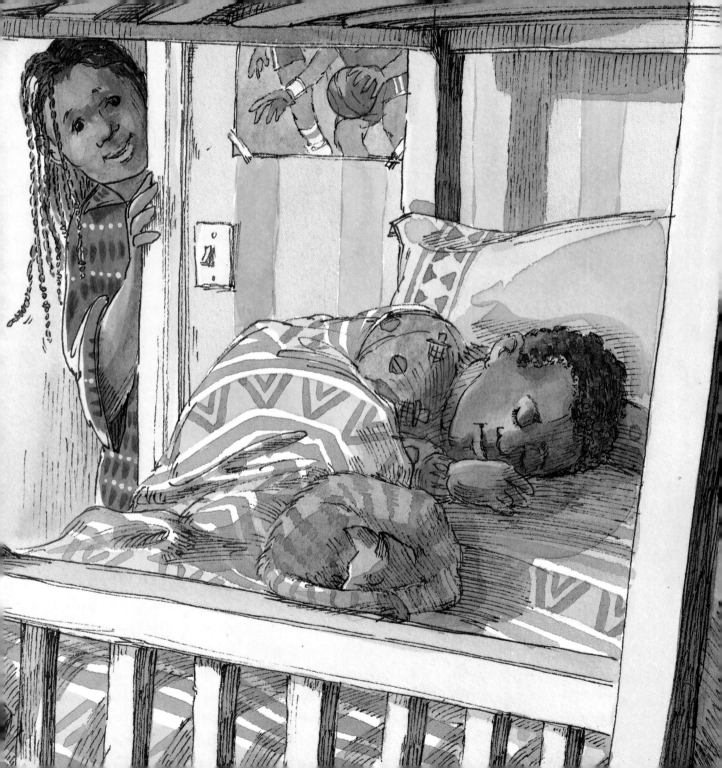

Birds chirp outside
my window as I dress
for school.

Pop!
Up springs my
toasted raisin bread.

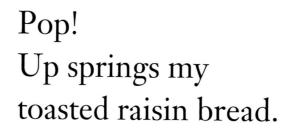

My sister's hair dryer
hums as she gets ready
for school.

The doors on the
school bus swish
as they open
and close.

The first school bell
rings as we hang up
our jackets.

Dad beeps the car horn
as he arrives home after
a long day's work.

A plate of food crashes onto the floor when my baby brother pushes it off the table.

The drinking glasses
clink as I help my dad
wash the dishes.

The water gurgles
as it drains from
the bathtub.

My kitten purrs
happily as we drift
off to sleep.

To Kent
—C.S.

For Peter L. Stevenson
—H.S.

SIMON & SCHUSTER BOOKS FOR YOUNG READERS
Simon & Schuster Building
Rockefeller Center
1230 Avenue of the Americas
New York, New York 10020
SIMON & SCHUSTER BOOKS FOR YOUNG READERS
is a trademark of Simon & Schuster.
The text for this book is set in Janson.
The illustrations were done in watercolor and ink.
Manufactured in the United States of America

10 9 8 7 6 5 4 3 2 1

Library of Congress Cataloging-in-Publication Data
Schoberle, Cecile.
Morning sounds, evening sounds/by Cecile Schoberle ;
illustrated by Harvey Stevenson.   p.   cm.
Summary: A child listens to a variety of sounds during the day,
from Mom's wake-up call to a kitten's bedtime purr.
[1. Sound—Fiction.]   I. Stevenson, Harvey, ill.   II. Title.
PZ7.S3647Mo   1994   [E]—dc20   93-16786   CIP
ISBN: 0-671-87437-3